LADYBIRD BOOKS

UK | USA | Canada | Ireland | Australia | India | New Zealand | South Africa

Ladybird Books is part of the Penguin Random House group of companies
whose addresses can be found at global.penguinrandomhouse.com.

www.penguin.co.uk   www.puffin.co.uk   www.ladybird.co.uk

Penguin
Random House
UK

First published 2022
001

Licensed by

Printed in China

The authorized representative in the EEA is Penguin Random House Ireland,
Morrison Chambers, 32 Nassau Street, Dublin D02 YH68

A CIP catalogue record for this book is available from the British Library

ISBN: 978–0–241–54349–8

All correspondence to:
Ladybird Books, Penguin Random House Children's
One Embassy Gardens, 8 Viaduct Gardens, London SW11 7BW

My Peppa Adventure

Look at the pictures on each page, and choose
your favourite ones to tell your own stories!

You're going on a brilliant adventure with Peppa! Where in the world do you want to go?

Which of Peppa's family and friends are you going to take with you on your adventure?

What will you and Peppa wear?

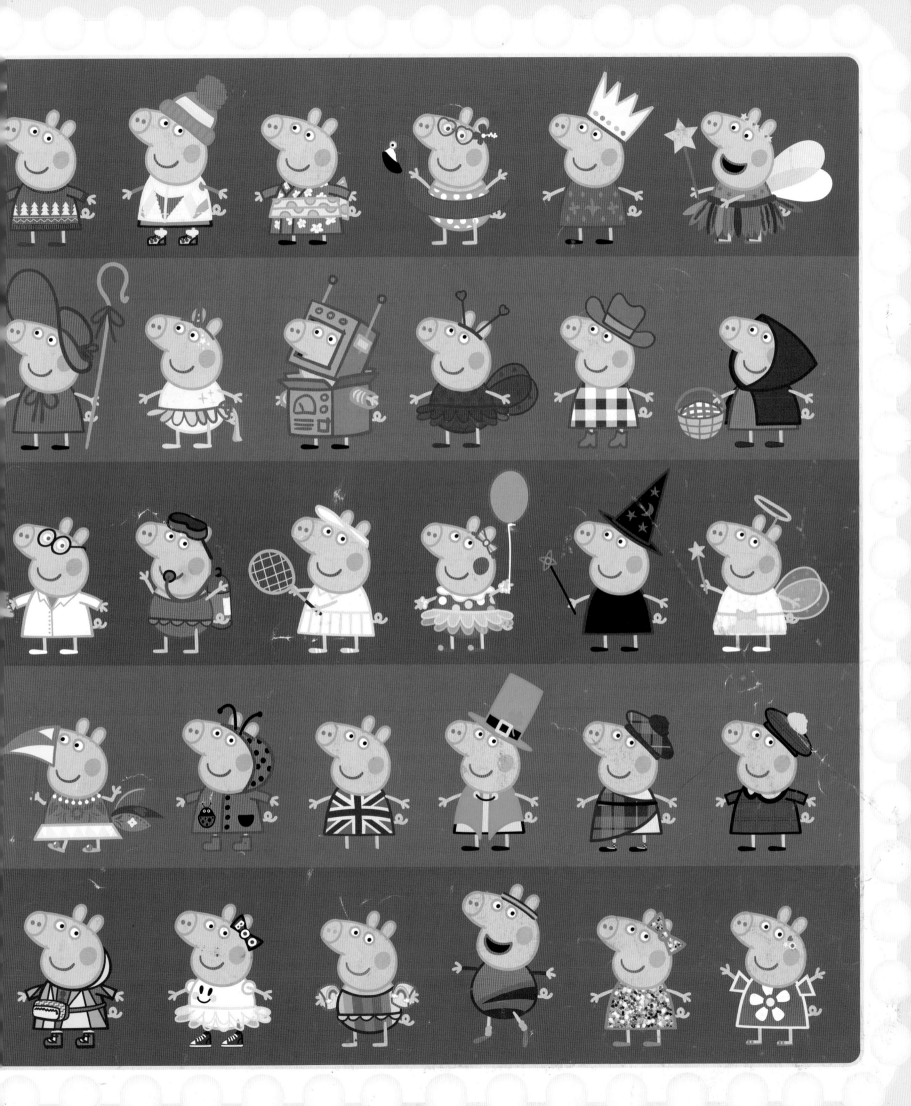

Mmmm, lunchtime!
What would you like
to eat with Peppa?

You're having a
playground adventure.
What will you do there?

If you could live anywhere
on your adventures, where
would you live?

Find a fun activity to do with Peppa! Which is your favourite?

Time to shop!

Which shop will you visit first?

POLICE

Pick a magical adventure
to have with Peppa!

Pick a party to go to with Peppa!

It's time for a work adventure!
Which job will you and Peppa do?

baker

nurse

biologist

detective

ballet dancer

footballer

artist

computer
scientist

doctor

basketball player

potter

ice-cream seller

police officer

zookeeper

astronaut

scuba diver

firefighter

builder

tennis player

yoga teacher

photographer

magician

ABC
abcdefghijklm
nopqrstuvwxyz

teacher

postal worker

scientist

swimmer

gardener

musician

Finally, choose a muddy puddle
to jump in with Peppa!

Goodbye!